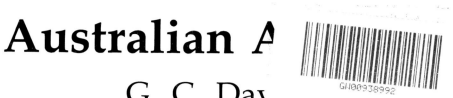

Australian A

G. C. Dav

Illustrated by Mike Dodd

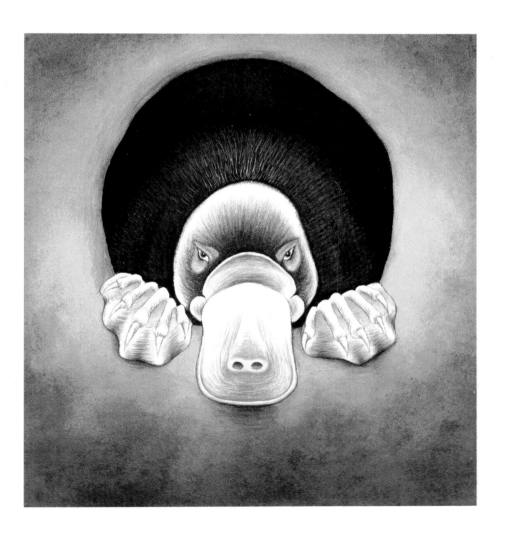

Basil Blackwell

KANGAROO

Good day!

Australians always say "Good day!"

I'm Australian.

I'm a young, red, girl **Kangaroo**

called Joey.

When I was born I was very tiny,

about as long as your

little finger.

I lived in my Mum's pouch for

sixteen weeks.

Her pouch is like a pocket on

her tummy.

It was great.

I had all my meals in bed.

All my meals were milk from my Mum.

No wonder I'm a big Joey!

I live with my family which
is called a mob.

My Dad is boss of our mob.

Our mob is always on the move.

We travel at night, when
it is cool.

We eat early in the morning
and late at night.
We eat plants and grass.
We can go without water for
a long time.
Farmers don't like us much.
We eat the grass meant for
their sheep and cattle.

You should see us jump.

My Dad can jump over a high fence.

My Dad's just great!

We use our back legs for jumping.

Our big tails help us keep our balance.

When kangaroos move slowly they
do not jump.
They go on all fours.
Perhaps I should say all fives,
because sometimes we lean on
our tails, too.

My Mum is called a blue flier.

She can move at 35 miles an hour.

My Mum's great, too!

All female kangaroos are

called blue fliers.

Even red kangaroos!

Men kangaroos sometimes fight and

wrestle with each other.

They hit each other with

their front paws.

They lean on their tails and

lash out with their big back legs.

Nasty.

I'm glad I'm a girl kangaroo.

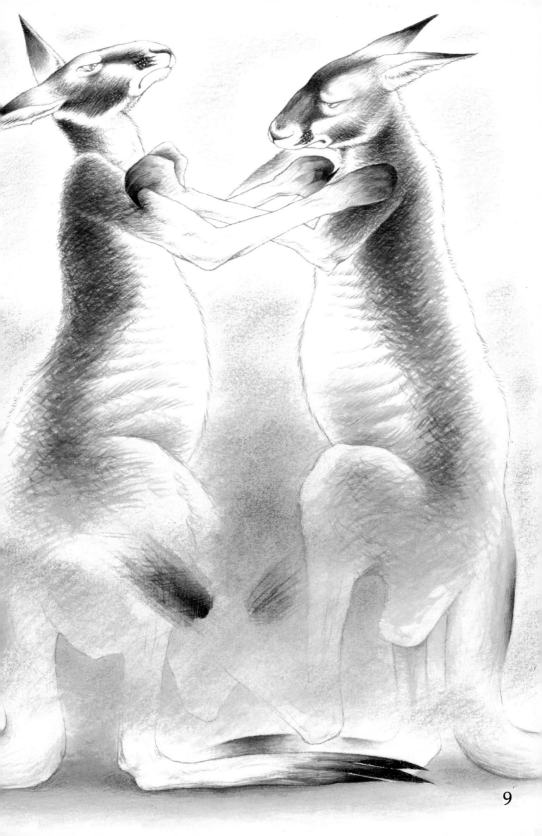

PLATYPUS

Good day!

Yes, I'm Australian too.

I'm a **Platypus**.

Now, a **mammal** is an animal that

has warm blood,

has hair or fur on its body,

feeds its babies on its

own milk

and has live babies.

I have warm blood.

I have fur on my body.

I feed my babies on my own milk, but

I lay eggs!

So am I a mammal?

Or what?

I'm a very odd mammal,

to be sure.

I have a bill, or beak, like

a duck.

So I am called a

duck-billed platypus.

I have feet like a duck, too.

My body is about 50 cm long.

I have a flat tail and

a coat of thick, soft fur.

A male platypus has spikes on
his back legs.

Nasty, aren't they?

The spikes have poison in them.

It can kill some small animals.

It would make **you** feel ill.

He does not use the spikes to
attack other animals.

He only uses them to look after himself.

I spend a lot of time
swimming in the river.
I eat little animals and worms
that live in the river.
I have pouches in my cheeks.
I use these to carry food back
to my nest.

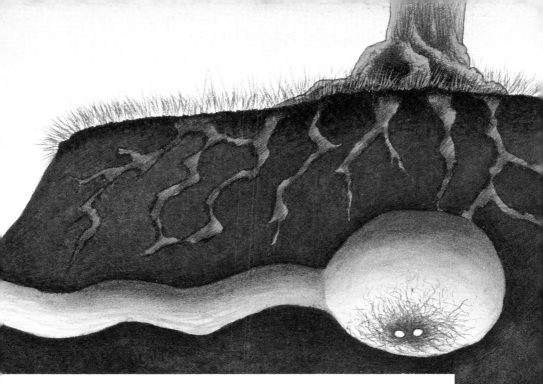

I make my nest of leaves and grass.

I make it in a round room, at

the end of a long tunnel under

the river bank.

I lay my eggs there.

I only lay two eggs.

They have soft shells.

They are about the size

of a sparrow's egg.

When they hatch out I feed

the babies with my own milk.

So I **must** be a mammal!